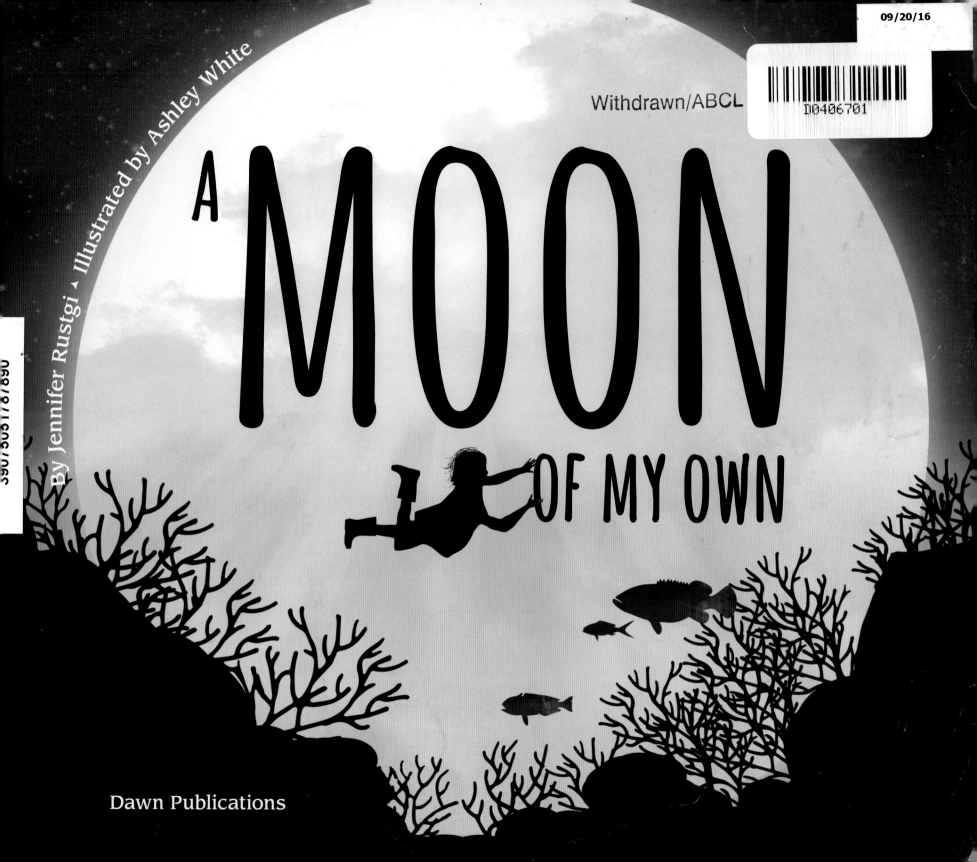

By Jennifer Rustgi ▴ Illustrated by Ashley White

A MOON

OF MY OWN

Dawn Publications

For Anjali. Never stop questioning. JR
For Avi. Adventures await. AW

Library of Congress Cataloging-in-Publication Data
Names: Rustgi, Jennifer, author. | White, Ashley, 1984- illustrator.
Title: A moon of my own / by Jennifer Rustgi ; illustrated by Ashley White.
Description: First edition. | Nevada City, CA : Dawn Publications, [2016] |
    Summary: "A young girl travels the world in a dream with her faithful
    companion, the moon, showing moon phases from iconic places on all seven
    continents. Includes resources and activities for teachers and facts about
    the moon and the places visited"-- Provided by publisher.
Identifiers: LCCN 2016000274| ISBN 9781584695721 (hardback) | ISBN
    9781584695738 (pbk.)
Subjects: | CYAC: Moon--Fiction.
Classification: LCC PZ7.1.R88 Mo 2016 | DDC [E]--dc23 LC record available at
http://lccn.loc.gov/2016000274

Prepress and computer production — Patty Arnold, *Menagerie Design & Publishing*

Manufactured by Regent Publishing Services, Hong Kong
Printed May, 2016, in ShenZhen, Guangdong, China
10 9 8 7 6 5 4 3 2 1
First Edition

Come along on an enchanted adventure around the world with a young girl and her faithful companion, the Moon.

Hey there, Moon. There you are again.

I wonder, why do you follow me?

Are you feeling lonely?

I can be your friend.

I love to go on adventures.

I think you do, too!

You must be very bright.

I never tell you where I'm going, but somehow you always find me.

Each night you seem a little different from the night before.

But I always know it's you.

Some nights you dart in and out of view.

Just when I think you don't
want to be found,

your light comes shining through.

Other nights you're bold and bright.

A spotlight in the darkness that makes hidden things appear.

One night you were so gigantic you seemed to swallow up the sky!

I felt like I could reach up and grab you.

But my favorite is when the sky comes alive with colors!

Do you do that? Just for me?

No matter how far away I go, you're right there with me.

And when I'm tired, you're there to guide me home.

I'm really lucky to have a Moon of my own.

Wonderful Places Around the World

Read about these wonderful places and match them to their locations on the world map on the facing page. Where in the world would you like to go?

The Eiffel Tower (Paris, France)

When this tower was built in 1889 it was only expected to last 20 years. But today it's one of the most visited tourist spots in the world. You can climb 1665 stairs to get to the top.

Trans-Siberian Railway (Russia)

This is the longest rail line in the world—6,000 miles long. That's 1/3 of the way around the world. A one-way trip takes 7 days.

Serengeti National Park (Africa)

Serengeti means "endless plain." This huge park is home to animals that live on Africa's savanna—lions, elephants, rhinos, gazelle, wildebeest, and many other species.

Great Wall of China (China)

This is the longest wall ever built— over 5,000 miles. It was built long ago to protect China from attacks and invasions. Over 7,000 lookout towers are part of the wall.

Taj Mahal (Agra, India)

The name Taj Mahal means "Crown of Palaces." It was built in memory of an Indian queen by her husband. The walls are made of white marble and gemstones.

Sequoia National Park (California, United States)

Sequoias are the world's largest single stem trees. They're so big that a car can drive through a tunnel in the tree's trunk. They're also one of the oldest things on Earth—3,500 years old.

Great Barrier Reef (Pacific Ocean near Australia)

This is the largest coral reef system in the world. It's so big it can even be seen from outer space! Over 1500 different types of fish live on this reef.

Amazon Rainforest (South America)

This rainforest contains more plant and animal species than any other ecosystem on Earth! The Amazon River that flows through it is one of the largest and longest rivers in the world.

Aurora Borealis (Arctic Circle)

This natural light show is also called the "Northern Lights." It appears at the Earth's North Pole.

Penguin Colony (Antarctica)

Thousands of Adelie penguins gather on the shores of Antarctica to nest. Their blubber keeps them warm at the coldest place on Earth— Antarctica, where the average temperature is minus 58° F.

Seven Continents of the World

Notice the Pattern

The Moon may seem to be changing its shape every night, but it's not. It only looks that way to us on Earth. We call the Moon's different shapes *phases*. The phases repeat in a continuous cycle. We can even predict what the Moon will look like next year or in the next 100 years.

Try this: Find the different phases of the Moon on the pages of the story. Compare them to the pattern below. All of the phases are shown the way they appear when looking at the Moon from the Northern Hemisphere, which includes the U.S. and Canada. You won't find a New Moon in the story. Can you figure out where in the story it would have occurred?

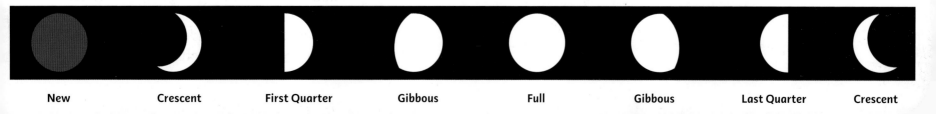

| New | Crescent | First Quarter | Gibbous | Full | Gibbous | Last Quarter | Crescent |

Children have a natural curiosity about the moon! Support this curiosity and encourage a deeper understanding about the Moon with the following information and activities.

Moon Matter of Facts

- **What:** The Moon is Earth's only natural satellite. It's made of various kinds of rock. Some planets don't have moons. Jupiter has over 60.

- **Distance:** The Moon is about 250,000 miles from Earth. Traveling by car, it would take you 174 days to drive that far. The Apollo spaceship took almost four days.

- **Size:** The diameter of the Moon is about one-quarter of the Earth's diameter. The surface of the Moon has about the same area as the continent of Africa.

- **Moon Phases:** The same amount of light from the Sun strikes the Moon all the time. Thus, every day half of the Moon is illuminated. The amount of the illuminated portion of the Moon that we see varies, depending on where the Moon is in its orbit of the Earth. When we see all of the illuminated half, we call it a Full Moon. When we see none of the illuminated half, we call it a New Moon.

Fact or Fiction—Getting the Answers

- **Why does it look like the Moon follows you?** This question by the author's young daughter inspired the writing of this book. Objects that are far away seem to stay in the same place even when you move.

- **Is the Moon bigger on some nights?** No. The Moon is always the same size. However, the Moon appears be larger when it is near the horizon. To notice this optical illusion, hold a nickel between thumb and forefinger at arm's length so that it just covers the Full Moon as it rises. Do the same a few hours later.

- **Can you only see the Moon at night?** No. It can also be seen during the day. Usually the Sun's light outshines other objects in the sky. But the Moon is relatively big, bright, and close to the Earth, so it may be visible during the day, depending on its phase.

- **Does the Moon cause the Aurora Borealis?** No. The Aurora Borealis is caused by the energy from the Sun interacting with the magnetic field and the Earth's atmosphere at the North and South Poles. The Aurora Borealis is usually seen in a striking green color, but very occasionally shows other colors.

- **Does moonlight shining into water make things appear?** It depends. The power of full moonlight shining through water is one million times less than the power of full sunlight.

- **Does the Moon look the same all around the Earth?** Yes and No. On any given night, the same Moon phase is seen all around the world. However, the waxing and waning phases look different in different hemispheres. In the Northern Hemisphere, the light of the waxing Moon is on the right side of the Moon, and the light of the waning Moon is on the left. In the Southern Hemisphere, it's just the opposite—when waxing, the light is on the left. When waning, the light is on the right.

Creating a Moon Phase Journal

Observing the Moon and keeping a journal of its changing phases is a fun activity that can involve the whole family.

- New Moon—The side of the Moon that is lighted doesn't face the Earth. But if you look closely, you may be able to see a tiny circle of light against the pitch black background of surrounding sky.

- Waxing Crescent—Most visible just before or a few minutes after sunset.

- First Quarter—Rises at noon and sets at midnight. Most visible around dusk. It can be seen all afternoon and evening.

- Waxing Gibbous—Visible most of the day and into the night.

- ◗ Full Moon—Visible from sunset to sunrise.

- ◗ Waning Gibbous—Visible most of the night and into the morning.

- ◗ Last Quarter—Rises at midnight and sets at noon. Most visible in dark sky before dawn.

- ◗ Waning Crescent—Most visible just before sunrise.

Activity: Have children keep a Moon Journal by observing the moon each day and drawing what it looks like. After one month, ask students to predict the phase for the next several days. Compare their predictions with how the moon actually looked.

Modeling the Moon

Unlike the Sun, the Moon does not create its own light. When we see the Moon "shining," what we're actually seeing is light from the Sun bouncing off the surface of the Moon. Moonlight is actually reflected sunlight.

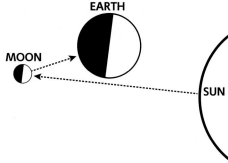

Demonstration—Part 1: Hold up a small ball. Ask children if the ball is making any light. (No) Turn on a flashlight and ask if it is making any light. (Yes) Tell children that the flashlight represents the Sun. The ball represents the Moon. Shine the flashlight on the ball. Ask children to imagine that they are observing the Sun and Moon from Earth. What do they see? (The Sun is shining on the Moon and making it brighter.) Draw the diagram on the board and relate it to the demonstration.

Demonstration—Part 2: Turn off the lights and shine the flashlight (Sun) on the ball (Moon) in the darkened room. Ask children what they notice. Turn the lights back on again to have children notice the difference. Explain that the Moon appears brighter in the night sky because the sky is dark. It's often possible to see the Moon in the day sky, but we usually don't notice it because the sky is bright.

Demonstration—Part 3: Watch the youtube video of author Emily Morgan demonstrating the phases of the moon using a lamp and a Styrofoam ball. You can do this demonstration yourself. nexttimeyousee.com/resources.html#moon

Moon Art

Artists have been inspired by the Moon for thousands of years. Ashley White, the illustrator of this book, created her illustrations in silhouette. A silhouette is an image of a person, object, or scene that is done in a solid color (usually black) that only shows the outline of that shape. Look back at the pages in the story to notice the silhouettes of people and places.

Activity: It can be challenging to make a silhouette that's recognizable to others. Begin with a simple object, person, or scene. Practice sketching the outline on white paper. For your final version, draw it on black construction paper. Cut out the silhouette and glue it onto lighter colored paper.

Recommended Resources

The Next Time You See the Moon by Emily Morgan (NSTA Kids)

Owl Moon by Jane Yolen (Philomel Books)

The Moon Book by Gail Gibbons (Holiday House)

NASA Kids' Club, www.nasa.gov

National Science Teachers Association, www.nsta.org

World MOON Project, www.worldmoonproject.org

Don't Miss It! There are many useful resources online for most of Dawn's books, including activities and standards-based lesson plans. Scan this code to go directly to activities for this book, or go to www.dawnpub.com and click on "Activities" for this and other books.

Jennifer Rustgi developed a love of children's literature during her years teaching reading as an elementary school teacher and became inspired to write her own stories through her experiences with her young daughter. The idea for *A Moon of My Own* grew out of her (then 3-year-old) daughter asking, "Mama, why does the Moon always follow me?" Jennifer lives in Austin, Texas, with her husband and daughter.

Ashley White is a graphic artist, illustrator, outdoor-fanatic, peony-gazer, and daydreamer, with an eye for all things fabulous and creative. Her illustrations for *A Moon of My Own* are inspired by her love of travel and her daughter who wears rain boots every day. When she is not exploring the world, she lives just outside of Austin, Texas, with her husband, daughter, and handsome dog, Tsavo.

More Books to Enjoy from Dawn Publications

Going Around the Sun: Some Planetary Fun—A rhymed tour of our solar system that explains the spin, tilt, sparkle, and whirl of our planetary neighbors.

If You Were My Baby—Here is a unique blend of love song and nonfiction that celebrates the care that exists between parents and their babies. For all generations of nature lovers.

The Dandelion Seed—Follow a dandelion seed on a journey that is sometimes challenging, sometimes wonderful, but always beautiful. Poetic and poignant.

Over in the Jungle: A Rainforest Rhyme—The rainforest is teeming with hooting monkeys, pouncing ocelots, squawking parrots, and so much more. One of many books in the "Over" series.

Over in the Arctic: Where the Cold Winds Blow—Children count, clap, and sing to the rhythm of "Over in the Meadow" as they learn about the animals that live where it's very, very cold.

On Kiki's Reef—Come along with Kiki, a green sea turtle, as she discovers the busy life of a coral reef, with all of its surprises! Complete with "Teaching Treasures" in the back.

Sunshine on My Shoulders—This adaptation of one of John Denver's best-loved songs celebrates friendship, sunshine, and simple joys.

Forest Night, Forest Bright—In this beautifully illustrated book, children meet a community of forest animals. Some are active during the day, others at night.

Dawn Publications is dedicated to inspiring in children a deeper understanding and appreciation for all life on Earth. You can browse through our titles, download resources for teachers, and order at www.dawnpub.com or call 800-545-7475.